The Birthday Hunt

Meet Leap's Friends

GO

Today
is your birthday.
Leap, open your eyes!
Today is the day of
your birthday
surprise!
Follow the riddles!
You'll need
them the most
to know where to go-
your first clue's
on toast!

STOP

Breakfast! You got it!
You're doing great!
Your present is waiting.
Don't want to be late.
So let's go to town.
There's so much to do.
And listen up, Leap!
Find the secret code clue!
6
1
JAM
2
7
5
4
10
8
3
9

GO
PARK
JUNK
STOP

You made it to town!
But no one's around.
Hmm. . .
Where do you think
the next clue
will be found?
Well,
where would you go
at the end of the day,
when school is all done,
and you just want to play?
ZOO
CANDY STORE

GO
5
1
2
3
4
11
12
13
14
15
one
two
three
four
five
eleven
twelve
thirteen
fourteen
fifteen
STOP

You're right! The park!
You've got a good mind!
Don't stop now -
there's a present to find!
Now, can you guess
where you'd go to rest
if your metal was crusty,
and friends called you Rusty?
6
7
8
9
10
16
17
18
19
20
six
seven
eight
nine
ten
sixteen
seventeen
eighteen
nineteen
twenty

GO
STOP

That's it! The junkyard!
Just the right spot!
The next clue is somewhere
in this crazy lot.
Look at the mountain
of junk by this riddle!
Which way is up?
Where is the middle?
OIL

PIZZA
GO
STOP

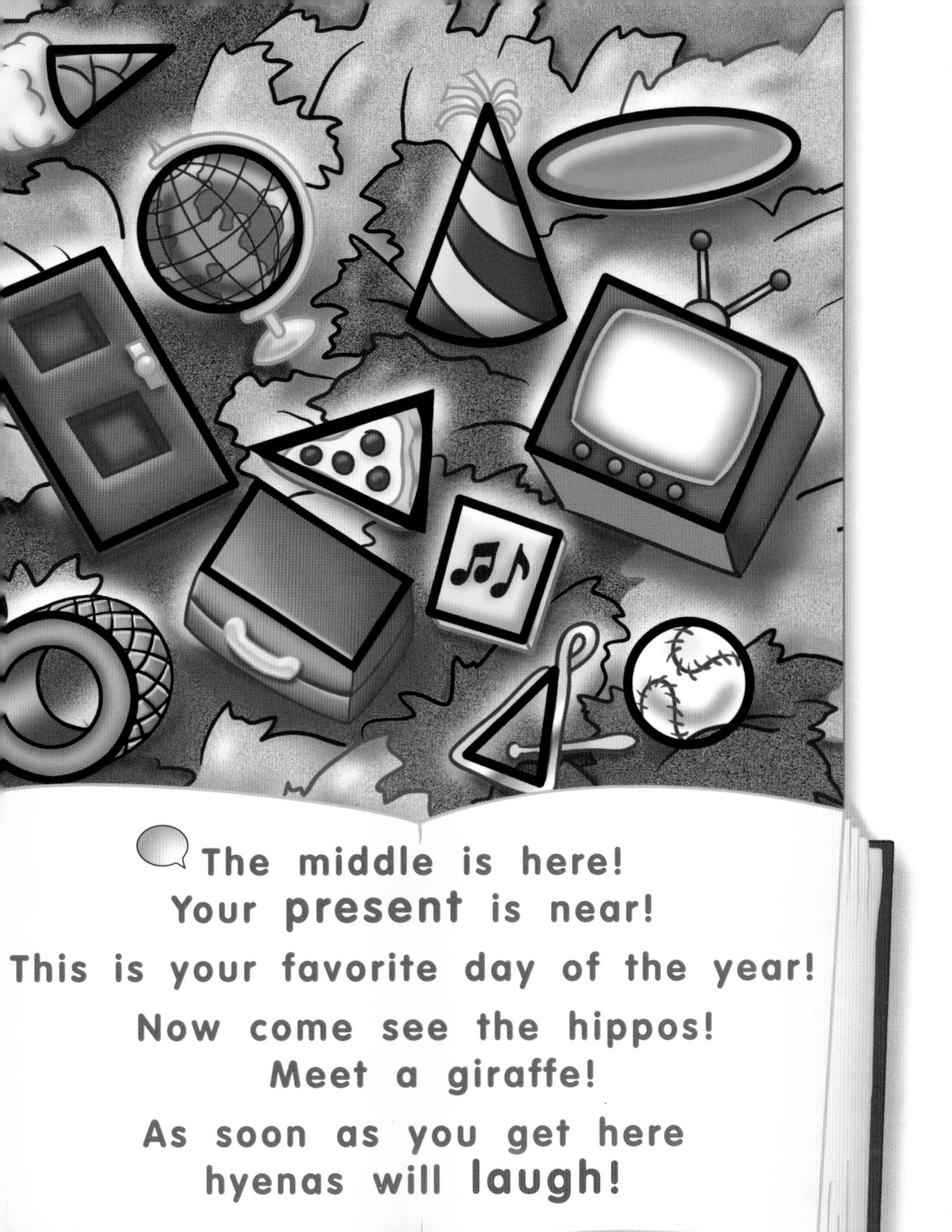

The middle is here!
Your **present** is near!
This is your favorite day of the year!

Now come see the hippos!
Meet a giraffe!

As soon as you get here
hyenas will **laugh**!

The zoo! The zoo!
I knew it would do!
Ready now, Leap,
for your next birthday clue?
People play music
right in this square.
Find the town band,
and you will be there!
GO
STOP

Animals
ZOO

GO
STOP

It's the town square!
You did it!
Now where?
Well, what it sells
is yummy
and shiny and sticky!
There's nothing
in here
that is
yucky or icky.

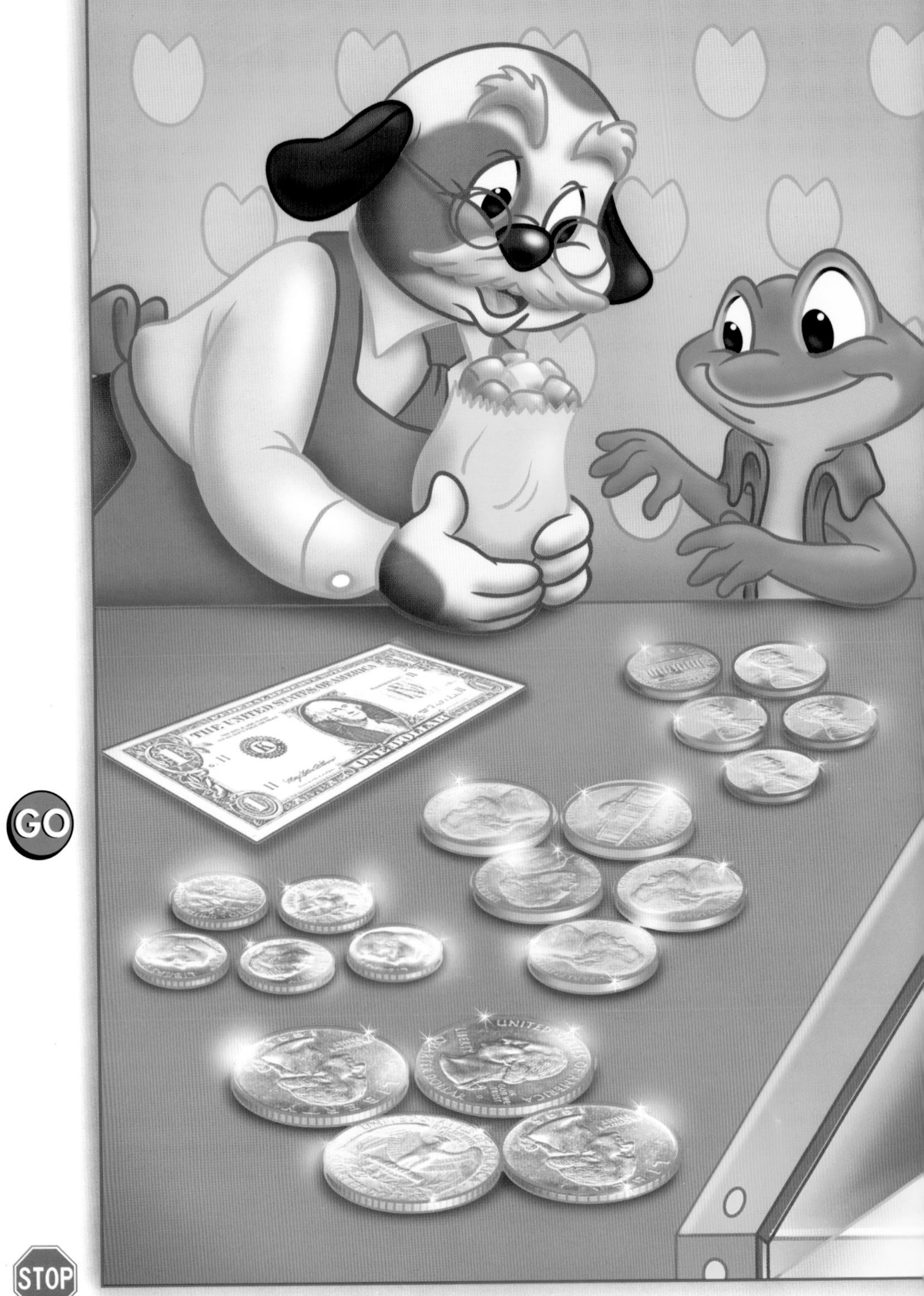
GO
STOP

The candy store! Yea!
You're well on your way!
The next clue is somewhere
you visit each day!
It's chock full of things.
They're just odds and ends,
but aren't they great
to show to your friends?

You made it
to the shop!
You're so close
I could **pop!**
You're getting warmer!
You're closer!
You're near!
1, **2, 3 steps,**
you're finally here!
GO
STOP

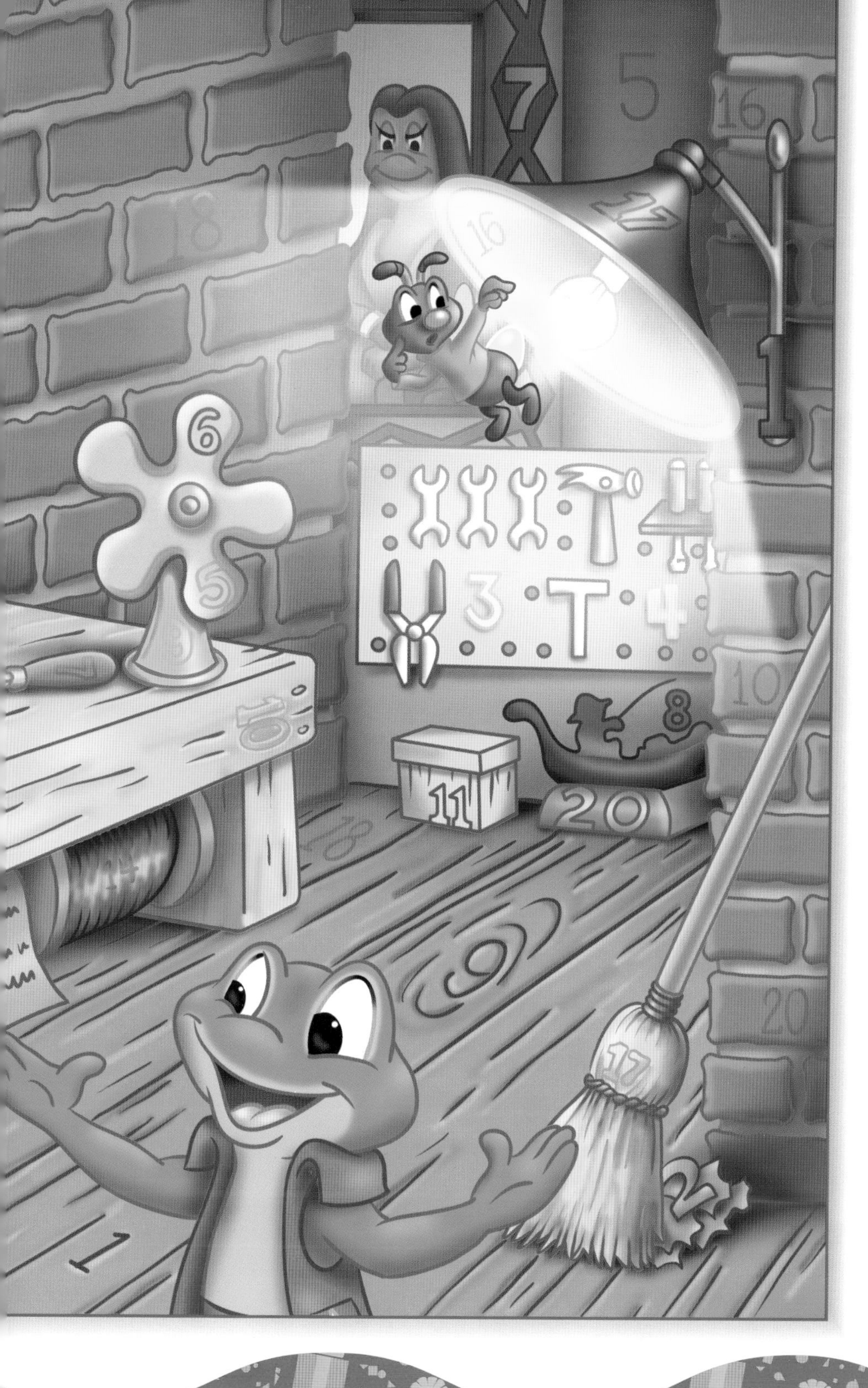

The back room!
Hooray!
And guess what we bought!
There's something in here
that you'll like a lot!
Now open the safe
with the clues that you got!
20
1
2
3
4
5
6
7
8
9
10
11
12
13
14
15
16
17
18
19
GO

STOP

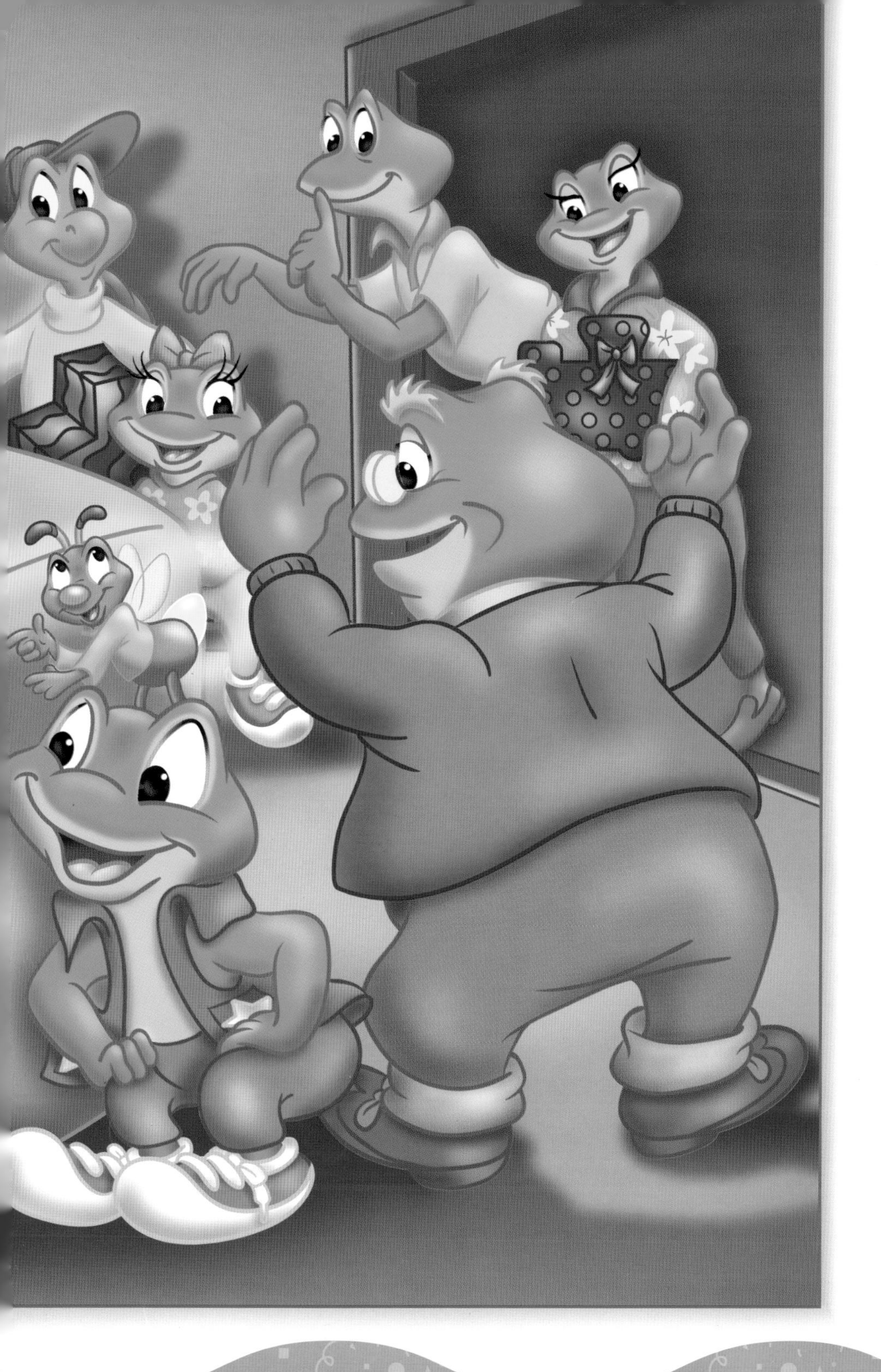

Lily
Mom and Dad
Edison
You did it! You got it!
And look - they're your size.
These new roller skates
are your **birthday surprise!**
Tim
Parker
tad
Grandpa
GO
STOP

GO

STOP